How to Be a Friend

by
Nancy Wilcox Richards

illustrations by
Annabelle Métayer

Scholastic Canada Ltd.
Toronto New York London Auckland Sydney
Mexico City New Delhi Hong Kong Buenos Aires

Scholastic Canada Ltd.
604 King Street West, Toronto, Ontario M5V 1E1, Canada

Scholastic Inc.
557 Broadway, New York, NY 10012, USA

Scholastic Australia Pty Limited
PO Box 579, Gosford, NSW 2250, Australia

Scholastic New Zealand Limited
Private Bag 94407, Botany, Manukau 2163, New Zealand

Scholastic Children's Books
Euston House, 24 Eversholt Street, London NW1 1DB, UK

Library and Archives Canada Cataloguing in Publication
Richards, Nancy Wilcox, 1958-
How to be a friend / by Nancy Wilcox Richards ;
illustrations by Annabelle Métayer.

ISBN 978-1-4431-0485-2

I. Métayer, Annabelle II. Title.

PS8585.I184H695 2011   jC813'.54   C2010-906023-7

6 5 4 3 2   Printed in Canada   121   13 14 15 16 17

MIX
Paper from
responsible sources
FSC® C004071

With love to Jenn, a paragon of kindness.

— N.W.R.

Chapter 1

Lexie Peters was scared. Well, maybe not scared, but nervous for sure. This was her third new school in two years. And it never got any easier. She had insisted that she could go down the hall and knock on the door to her Grade Three classroom all by herself.

"Are you sure you don't want me to come with you?" her dad had asked for the second time.

"I'm sure," Lexie had answered in a wobbly voice. Only babies had their parents walk them into school.

Now, as she knocked on the door, she

wished that her dad was standing right beside her. She took a deep breath and waited.

It seemed to take forever until her teacher, Ms Sampson, answered the door. "You must be Lexie," she said. "Welcome to Malone Bay Public School. Come in!" She waved her into the classroom, making the bracelets on her wrist jingle. Ms Sampson faced the class. "Boys and girls, we have a new student joining us." She smiled at Lexie. "This is Lexie Peters. She just moved here from Lunenburg."

Lexie felt everyone staring at her. Twenty pairs of curious eyes. She lowered her head and fiddled with the zipper on her jacket. She didn't dare look up. This school would be just like the last one. And then she heard the first whispers. Again. She couldn't make out what the other kids were saying, but she knew they were talking about her.

"You can sit here with Taylor and Gaven," directed Ms Sampson. She pointed to the empty chair at the table.

Lexie slid into the seat.

"Now, as I was just saying, this year our class will be doing a very special project," Ms Sampson said. "I hope you all will enjoy it. We'll be doing random acts of kindness for the who-o-o-le year." She stretched out the word "whole" to make it sound long. "Does anyone want to make a guess what that means?"

Lexie peeked around the room. Lots of kids had their hands up.

Ms Sampson looked at the freckly, red-haired boy at the back of the room. "Garrett, what do you think it means?"

"We'll treat everyone nice for the whole year," he guessed.

Ms Sampson smiled. "I like the way you think. But that's not quite it. Yes, we will be treating people kindly. But think about the word 'random.' What does that mean?"

When no one could guess the meaning, Ms Sampson said, "Random means you pick by chance. You will do something kind for someone else. It might be a friend. It might be a neighbour." She paused and smiled. "It could even be a complete stranger. The whole point is to make somebody's day a little bit better. A little brighter. But there's a tricky part." She looked at the class and grinned. "Are you up for a challenge?"

Lexie looked around the room. Heads were nodding up and down.

"You *can't* let the person know — at least, not until after it's done. Maybe never! You have to do it secretly. That'll be the tricky part." Ms Sampson laughed. "And it will make it more fun."

The teacher snapped her fingers as though she had just remembered something. "I almost forgot this." She pulled a smooth, grey stone out of her pocket. She held it up for everyone to see. "This is the kindness stone.

Whoever has the stone has to do the random act of kindness. You have just one week to do your good deed. Then you pass the stone on to someone else in the classroom."

Lexie looked at the kindness stone. It was small — about the size of quarter — and could easily fit into a pocket. Her heart felt heavy, like a stone. She frowned. She lowered her head and listened to the other kids talk excitedly about the project. She wished she knew someone to talk to. She wished she didn't have to do a random act of kindness. She really wished it didn't have to be secret. That was going to be a problem — a big problem. For Lexie, it would be just about impossible.

Chapter 2

"Boys and girls," said Ms Sampson, "take a few minutes and discuss the project with the people at your table. Let's see what ideas you can come up with."

There was a buzz throughout the room. Everyone seemed to have an idea. Everyone except Lexie.

She listened to Gaven and Taylor talk about the project. "I think I'm going to set the table for supper. That way my mom won't have to do it when she gets home from work," began Taylor. "She's always tired. And she won't be able to guess if it was me or one of my brothers who did it. Or maybe I could tidy the playroom." She began talking faster. "Or I could walk Mr. Stewart's dog. Surprise my

7

leaves or . . ." Taylor paused to
Gee, I could do anything! What are
ing to do, Gaven?"

Gaven's forehead wrinkled in concentration. "I'm not sure," he answered. "How do we keep it a secret? And what happens if you have the stone and a week goes by and you haven't done something nice yet? This sounds hard." He sighed as his shoulders slumped forward.

Taylor looked at Lexie. "What about you? Do you have any ideas about doing nice stuff for people?"

Lexie wanted to say something. Anything. Really, she did. But when she opened her mouth, the words just wouldn't come out. She glanced at Taylor. She seemed nice, and Lexie hoped that maybe, just maybe, she and Taylor could become friends. But right now, it was too hard to talk to someone she didn't know. "Um," she mumbled, "um . . . I'm not sure."

"Boys and girls, it's time for recess." Ms Sampson interrupted the class. She looked over at Lexie and smiled. "I wonder if Taylor and Gaven might like to show our new student around the playground this morning. Make sure she has someone to play with. Show her where the playground equipment is stored."

Taylor beamed. "Sure." She turned and faced Lexie. "Let's get ready for outside. We have the best monkey bars."

Lexie stayed in her seat. She clutched her stomach. "I don't feel good," she said. "I think I'd better stay inside."

Ms Sampson walked over and knelt down beside Lexie. She had a concerned look on her face. "What's wrong?" she asked.

"I don't feel good," Lexie repeated. "My tummy hurts."

Ms Sampson looked surprised. "Well, maybe it's a little case of nerves. Would you like to stay inside? Taylor could stay with you and that way you'll get to know her a bit better. The two of you can get out a game. How does that sound?"

Lexie smiled at her teacher. "That sounds good."

* * *

After recess, Ms Sampson said that it was time to give the kindness stone to the first person. "Who would like to go first?" she asked.

"Me!"

"Me!"

"Pick me!"

Almost everyone wanted to go first. Ms

Sampson looked around the room. She laughed. "You are all so keen! Emma, how about you?" She handed the stone to a girl sitting by the computer.

"Thanks," Emma replied. She turned the stone over and over before she tucked it in her pocket.

"Now remember," said Ms Sampson, "you have one week to do your act of kindness. You need to have the stone back by next Monday — sooner if you wish."

"No problem," Emma answered. "I know just what I want to do!"

The rest of the morning zipped by. Before Lexie knew it, it was time for lunch.

The cafeteria at Malone Bay Public School was big and noisy. Classes were sitting at long tables. Everyone seemed to be talking at once. Some kids ordered the daily special, veggie pizza. Most were unpacking lunch boxes, laying out their food.

Lexie sat next to Taylor. She watched as Taylor neatly lined up her food — a bagel with some kind of filling, apple juice and orange wedges. Then Taylor pulled out two humongous chocolate chip cookies. They looked delicious. Lexie could feel her mouth beginning to water.

Taylor held out a cookie. "Here," she said, "try one of my mom's cookies. They're the best. She puts tons of chocolate chips in them."

"No, thanks," answered Lexie. "I'm not allowed."

"Sure you can," replied Taylor. "My mom won't mind. That's why she always packs two. One for me. And one for a friend."

Lexie shook her head sadly. "I can't," she repeated, as she looked longingly at the cookies.

Taylor had a puzzled look on her face. Lexie knew she had to be wondering why she wouldn't take one. After all, the cookies would be so delicious — loaded with chocolate chips. Lexie sighed and began to unpack her lunch. Out of the corner of her eye, she saw Taylor looking at the tiny cut-up hot dogs, her special Jell-O, and other bits of food she knew her friend wouldn't recognize. She would be thinking this was really weird. Lexie stared at her lunch for a long time before she started to eat.

Chapter 3

After lunch was the best part of the day. Lots of time to play in the schoolyard. One minute Lexie seemed fine. The next minute she was claiming her tummy hurt. Again.

"But Lexie," Ms Sampson said, "you seemed fine just a minute ago in the cafeteria."

"I know," answered Lexie, "but the pain came back. I think I need to stay in again. And . . ." She paused and rubbed her forehead. "I have a headache, too."

"Really," said Ms Sampson, and Lexie knew by the way she said it that the teacher did not believe her. She eyed Lexie closely. "Is everything all right?"

Lexie's face reddened. The words seemed

to stick in her throat. "I . . . I . . . I . . . just don't feel . . . good . . ." she stammered.

Ms Sampson patted her shoulder. "There, there. It'll get better."

"Maybe." Lexie shuddered. "Maybe . . . Taylor . . . could stay . . . with me again. To keep me company."

"I think that's a wonderful idea," Ms Sampson said gently. She glanced over at Taylor. "Would you like to do that?"

"Sure," replied Taylor. She wrapped an arm around Lexie's shoulder. "Let's sit on the Comfy Couch." She pointed to a small couch at the back of the room. It was lined with red, yellow and blue pillows. In the middle was a huge teddy bear.

Taylor led Lexie to the back of the room. "I used to get headaches, too," she confided. "But then I got my glasses. Maybe you need glasses." She looked at Lexie hopefully.

Lexie thought about that. "Maybe," she said slowly. After a long time she said, "I really miss my old school. And my best friend, Maddie."

She sniffed and wiped her eyes on her sleeve. "I don't have any friends here."

Taylor looked at her and smiled. "I'll be your friend," she said.

Lexie smiled back. "Thanks."

* * *

But even though Lexie now had a friend, the same thing happened every day. Whenever it was time to go out for recess, she either had a headache, a pain in her tummy, or something else wrong with her. She always stayed inside. It happened on Tuesday. It happened again on Wednesday.

Thursday it rained. Friday it rained even harder. That meant an indoor recess for all the kids at Malone Bay Public School. Lexie happily played Lego with Gaven. She made books on the computer with Emma. It was fun!

"No pains today?" asked Ms Sampson.

Lexie smiled. "Nope," she answered. "I feel great!"

"I'm so glad," Ms Sampson said. "Maybe you had a little flu bug."

* * *

But the next week it was the same thing. Monday was a beautiful autumn day. When Ms Sampson announced, "It's time for recess, class. Put your math books away and let's head outside for some fresh air," Lexie was sick again.

She clutched her stomach. "I can't. I think

I'm going to barf." She looked at Ms Sampson, her eyes filled with tears.

"Lexie," said Ms Sampson sternly. "This is happening too much. Every time we have an outdoor recess, you are sick. You need to at least *try* to go outside. It'll be fun. You'll see."

But Lexie knew deep down that it would not be fun. It never was. Some kid would laugh at her. Another kid would tease her. She just knew it.

"We'll stay with her," Gaven spoke up. He pointed to himself and Taylor. "We'll make sure she's okay." He turned to Lexie. "Come on. It will be fun."

Lexie hung her head. Slowly she walked out of the classroom. She put on her jacket. She glanced up and down the hallway. Then she did something strange. She put on a bicycle helmet.

Taylor and Gaven looked at each other. Everybody knew you couldn't ride bikes on the playground at recess time. "Um, you're

not allowed to ride your bike right now,"
Taylor explained.

"I know," Lexie answered unhappily.

Mr. Johnson, the playground helper, was
waiting at the doors at the end of the hallway.
That was strange, too.

Mr. Johnson took a good look at Lexie's sad face. He eyed her purple helmet with the butterfly stickers plastered all over it. "You must be Lexie," he said. "I was beginning to think I'd never get to meet you. I'm your playground helper." He smiled. "Let's go outside. It's a fabulous day!"

Gaven whispered to Taylor, "Playground helper? Why does Lexie need a playground helper?"

Taylor shrugged her shoulders. "I don't know. It's kind of weird."

Chapter 4

"Hey, Lexie!" Gaven said, once they were outside. "What's going on?" He pointed to the helmet. "How come you're wearing that? We told you, no biking at recess time." He looked over at Mr. Johnson. "And why is Mr. Johnson with you?"

"I have to wear it. And he has to be around." Then, so quietly that it was hard to hear her, she added, "Because I have epilepsy." She held up her wrist and gave a silver bracelet a little shake. "See? It tells you on here." For the second time that morning, her eyes filled with tears. "All I want is to be like everyone else. Everywhere I go, I'm different. I just want to be normal."

"Epilepsy?" Taylor said. "What's that? Is a disease?"

"Not exactly," admitted Lexie. "It's a condition that causes seizures."

"What are they?" asked Taylor.

"When I have a seizure, I shake. Sometimes, if it's really bad, I fall down. I can't help it. It's all because my brain gets a mixed-up message." She looked over at Mr. Johnson. "That's why I have a teacher helper when I'm out on the playground. In case I have a seizure. And it's the reason I have to wear this stupid helmet. If I fall and hit my head . . ." she trailed off.

"Bummer," said Taylor.

Gaven looked worried. "Can I catch it?"

"No," answered Lexie, "it's not contagious."

Gaven looked relieved but, at the same time, sad for his new friend. "I moved last year — all the way from Ontario. It was really hard. But this would be a lot worse." He smiled at Lexie. "How about we climb on the monkey bars?" he asked. "Race you!" he yelled, as he tore off across the playground.

"Wait for us!" called Taylor.

Swinging across the monkey bars was fun.

Out of the corner of her eye, Taylor noticed a bunch of kids huddled together near the swing set. They were pointing at Lexie. And they were laughing. Taylor was pretty sure they weren't laughing at any joke. She only hoped Lexie wouldn't notice them, too.

"Hey, Helmet Head!" called the biggest boy in the group.

Taylor dropped to the ground and looked at the big kids. She looked over at Lexie. Lexie had stopped climbing the monkey bars and was perched on the middle rung. She was clinging there as if her life depended on it. Her eyes looked sad.

"Hey, Helmet Head!" repeated the boy. "Did you forget something . . . like your bike? Or do you always go around looking like an idiot?" He turned to his friends and laughed.

"I hate those guys," Gaven muttered to Taylor. He nodded toward Lexie. "Bet she does, too." He scowled. Then he faced the bigger boy and shouted, "Leave her alone!"

"Mr. Johnson will do something," Taylor said.

Mr. Johnson was already marching over to the swings. He stopped next to the big kids. Taylor couldn't hear much of what he was saying. He was shaking a finger and talking in a stern voice. She heard a few of the words — "different," "treat others" and "principal's office." She glanced up at Lexie. "Let's go play somewhere else," she suggested.

Lexie nodded and slowly climbed down the monkey bars.

* * *

After recess, Ms Sampson faced the class. "Boys and girls," she began, "today we will hear about our first good deed. Emma is ready to talk about her random act of kindness, and to pass on the kindness stone. I can't wait to find out what she did." She clapped her hands together in excitement. Her bracelets jingled back and forth.

"I thought we weren't supposed to tell," Katherin said. "Isn't it supposed to be a secret?"

"Well, yes." Ms Sampson paused. "But I

meant it should be secret for the person who receives the act of kindness. And after you do your good deed, you can tell that person if you want." She looked at Emma. "Plus, I'm sure the whole class is excited to hear what Emma did."

Emma grinned. She turned the stone over and over in her hand. "On the weekend, I went shopping with my mom. Just as we were leaving Wilson's Mini Mart, I saw a man unlocking his car. When he pulled his keys out of his pocket, some money fell on the ground.

It was really windy and the money started blowing down the sidewalk. I ran after it. I had to run a whole block but I finally grabbed it! When I got back, the car was gone. So I left the money with the store lady. She said she knew the guy who lost it. He's in her store every day. And she would make sure he got his money back."

"That's wonderful, Emma!" Ms Sampson said. "I bet you felt great after doing your act of kindness."

"I did," Emma agreed. "And guess how much money it was?" She didn't wait for Ms Sampson to answer her. "Twenty dollars! That man is going to be so happy."

"What a terrific way to start our project," said Ms Sampson. "So," she continued, "Emma, you get to pick who will go next."

Emma looked around the room. Almost everyone's hand was up.

"Pick me, Emma."

"Pick me!"

"I want a turn."

"I pick . . . I pick . . ." She looked around the room. "Brady." Emma handed the kindness stone to the boy sitting near the teacher's desk.

Brady grasped the stone tightly in his fist. "I don't know what I'm going to do," he admitted. "But it will be fun just thinking about it!"

"Now, Grade Three, it's time for music," Ms Sampson announced. "Everybody line up."

The day seemed to fly by. Math, spelling, science — and then it was time for the bus. Ms Sampson took Lexie aside before she joined the bus line. "I've been thinking," she said in a low voice, "that it might be a good idea for you to talk to the class about epilepsy. Maybe do a little presentation. It would help everyone understand it a little bit better." She looked directly into Lexie's worried blue eyes. "What do you think?"

Lexie's shoulders slumped. There it was again. Epilepsy. All she really wanted was to be like everyone else. Doing a presentation would definitely make her stand out. Once again, she would be different. The kids would think she was weird.

"Maybe . . ." she answered.

"Just give it some thought," Ms Sampson said.

"Sure," Lexie mumbled. She fastened her helmet and trudged out to the bus. She didn't talk to anyone the whole way home.

Chapter 5

On Tuesday morning Lexie told Ms Sampson that her father thought it was a good idea to do the presentation, too. "He said he could come in on Friday to help me. We could talk about epilepsy together," she said.

"I think that's a marvellous idea," said Ms Sampson. "Friday it is."

* * *

When Friday rolled around, Lexie stood at the front of the room, feeling very nervous. Her stomach had butterflies and her hands were sweaty. She quickly glanced at all the kids in her class. They looked friendly and interested. She tried to relax.

Her dad started the presentation. "Thanks for letting Lexie and me tell you a bit about epilepsy," he began. He smiled at his daughter and then at the class. He rubbed his hands together. "Now, to start things off, Lexie has a game for you." He pointed to the poster his daughter held. "This will tell you a lot about the condition. And you can keep it for the classroom, if you'd like." He looked at Lexie. "Ready?"

Lexie took a deep breath. "You all know that I have epilepsy. But you probably don't know that I didn't always have it." She saw the surprised look on Gaven's face. "I was diagnosed with epilepsy when I was four years old. I've had it for almost four years." She looked over at her dad. "Dad helped me make a game to teach you about epilepsy." She pointed to the poster. "There are ten True or False questions. Every time you answer one right, the class scores a point." She smiled shyly at her classmates. "The correct answers are under these flaps of paper." She pointed to ten coloured pieces of paper glued to the chart. "Okay?"

"Yes! Let's get started!" Brady shouted.

"Number one," Lexie began. "Epilepsy is contagious."

"I know! I know that one!" yelled Gaven.

Lexie smiled. She remembered Gaven asking her that question just last week. "Gaven?"

"That's false."

"Correct. That's one point." Lexie lifted the flap and read, "You cannot catch epilepsy from another person." She faced her father. "Dad, would you keep score on the board?"

"Sure." He put a giant tally mark on the blackboard.

"Number two: True or false — Seizures happen when the brain gets a sudden burst of electricity."

Michael frantically waved his arm in air.

"Michael?"

"I think that's false," he answered. "You don't need to be around a plug or a cord or anything electrical to have a seizure."

"Actually that's true. But it's not that kind of electricity. It's a different kind." Lexie lifted the second flap and read, "Seizures happen when there is unusual electrical activity in your brain. This makes your body do things you can't control — like shaking, or falling asleep for a little while." Lexie looked at Michael. "Sorry, no point for that one."

She glanced around the classroom. "This next one is pretty tricky: People who have epilepsy can only work at easy jobs."

Slowly Hannah raised her hand. "I think that's false. I think they can do anything they want to."

"You're correct," answered Lexie. "Score another point, Dad." Lexie read from the poster, "People with epilepsy can do all kinds of different jobs. They might be actors, doctors, plumbers — even teachers." Lexie smiled at Ms Sampson.

Lexie continued quizzing the Grade Three class. Most times they got the answer right. The class had a total of seven points. "Now for the final question: You can only control epilepsy by taking medicine."

Brady whispered to Tyler, "I think that's true. What do you think?"

Tyler shrugged his shoulders. "I don't know."

Everyone whispered back and forth.

"That's true."

"No, it's not."

"True."

"False."

Taylor looked at her friend Lexie, her forehead scrunched in concentration. She was trying to remember something. But what was it? Somehow she knew the answer to this question. Then she remembered! "I know!" she yelled. "I'm sure I know the answer!"

Lexie looked surprised. "What do you think, Taylor? Can you only control epilepsy by taking medicine?"

"I think that's false," Taylor answered. "I think the reason you won't eat my mom's chocolate chip cookies is because you need to eat special foods."

"You're right!" said Lexie. She lifted the last flap. "Sometimes medicine doesn't work. Sometimes kids need to have a special diet called a ketogenic diet." She looked at the class. "I can only eat certain foods. Sometimes it's hard. Really hard. If I go to a birthday party, I can't have a piece of birthday cake."

All of the kids looked sad. No one could imagine never eating birthday cake.

Lexie smiled. "I haven't had a seizure for almost a whole year. And that's really good news." She glanced at the score. Her dad had tallied eight points. That was more good news.

Her dad spoke, "Grade Three, thank you for being such great listeners. Lexie and I have a little something for you."

Lexie handed out stickers to the class. There was a purple ribbon shaped like a butterfly on each one.

"Cool!" said Emma.

Lexie smiled at her dad. She knew the kids now understood epilepsy a little bit better. I hope I'll never be called Helmet Head again, she thought, crossing her fingers. But deep down inside, she wasn't too sure.

Chapter 6

"Thank you so much for teaching all of us about epilepsy today," said Ms Sampson. The class was lining up for gym. "*I* even learned a thing or two." She paused. "I didn't know Beethoven had epilepsy. Or Agatha Christie, one of my favourite authors." She smiled at Lexie. "Now, don't forget you'll need your helmet for gym."

Lexie walked out into the hall. She grabbed her helmet and joined the end of the line. She was still thinking about her presentation. Everybody had liked it. The whole class had been surprised to learn that even animals can have epilepsy. I did okay, she thought. But still, she wished she didn't have to wear the dumb helmet. She might as well have a big neon sign flashing above her head saying, "Look how different I am." She frowned.

Taylor touched her arm. "What's wrong?" she asked.

"This." Lexie tapped her helmet. "Plus, I keep thinking, what if I *do* have a seizure? It's been a long time, but still . . ."

"It's okay," said Taylor. "You have lots of friends now. We know what to do if it happens. We'll look after you."

"Thanks." Lexie smiled. She pointed to the gym teacher. "Look, Mrs. MacDonald has hula hoops. I bet that's what we're doing in gym!"

"Good morning, everyone!" said Mrs. MacDonald. "It's such a beautiful day that we are going to have our gym class outdoors today. And we'll be using these." She held up a bundle of hula hoops. "We'll also be partnering with the other Grade Three class today. Let's head out!"

"I love hula hooping," said Lexie.

"Not me," Emma said. "I can never get it to stay up."

"Me neither," said Gaven. "I was hoping we might use the scooters today."

Once the two classes were outside and everyone had a hoop, Mrs. MacDonald yelled, "Boys and girls, space out! Give yourselves lots of room!"

Lexie swung the hoop around her hips. She began counting, "One, two, three . . ." as it spun around and around. ". . . twenty-eight, twenty-nine . . . thirty."

Gaven watched closely. He swung the hoop the same way as Lexie. It made one turn and crashed to the ground. He tried it again. Another turn. Crash to the ground. Again and again Gaven tried to hula hoop. Each time the hoop circled his waist once and then fell to the ground.

"Try bending your knees a bit more," Lexie encouraged.

"I can't do it," he moaned.

"Well, look who's here," said a loud voice. "It's Helmet Head. And she's giving lessons on hula hooping."

Lexie had only heard that voice once before but she knew right away who it belonged to. It was the big kid from the playground. The one who had teased her the very first time she went on the monkey bars. It was just her luck that he was in the other Grade Three class.

"You look like you're having a fit." He

laughed in a mean way. "You're wobbling all over the place. You look like a bowlful of jelly." He laughed again.

Lexie's heart began to pound. She was afraid to look at him. If only she didn't have to wear the helmet. Then she would be like everybody else. Nobody would make fun of her.

"Hey, leave her alone!" shouted Gaven. "I bet she can hula hoop waaaaay better than *you*!"

The big kid looked surprised. "Whatever," he said, and he stalked off to the other side of the playground.

Gaven put down his hoop. He walked over to Lexie. "Are you okay?" he asked. "He's such a bully. Anyway, you're the best hula hooper in the class. Just look around." He waved his arm at all the other kids.

Lexie looked around the playground. A few kids knew how to do it. Most were like Gaven. The hoop took a couple of spins and then fell to the ground. Lexie knew she was good at this. But right now, all she could think about were the words, "You look like you're having a fit." That's what some people said about epilepsy.

Chapter 7

On Monday, the entire class was excited to hear about Brady's random act of kindness.

"So," Ms Sampson began, "it was your turn to do a good deed, Brady. What did you manage to do?"

Brady smiled. "At first I wasn't sure what to do. I thought about sweeping out the garage. Then I thought about unloading the dishwasher for a whole week. I even thought about cleaning the fish tank. Doing that is such a pain. But none of those things seemed just right. Then, the perfect opportunity came along.

"Yesterday," he continued, "I went to the park with my family. Just like we always do. My sister and I were playing on the teeter-totters. I noticed there was a lot of litter on the ground. So when we were finished playing, I picked it all up. It's like doing something nice for everyone who uses the park. And no one will ever know that I did it."

Ms Sampson beamed. "That's wonderful. I'm sure everyone in Malone Bay who uses the park will appreciate that. Now you get to pass the stone to someone else."

Brady looked at his classmates. Lots of kids were waving their arms in the air.

"Pick me!"

"I want a turn!"

Lexie looked around the room. It seemed like everyone wanted to be next. Everyone knows what they are going to do, she thought. Everyone but me. Lexie did not raise her hand.

Brady wasn't sure who he should give the stone to. "Soheil, do you want it?"

"Yes!" Soheil was bouncing out of his seat. He took the stone and rubbed it. "This will be fun!"

* * *

The rest of Monday was pretty ordinary — writers' workshop, math, spelling and reading. On Tuesday it was the same — more math, more spelling and more reading. That is, until it was time for lunch.

As usual, Lexie sat next to Emma and Taylor. She was busy spreading out her lunch when she heard that voice again. "Guess I'll have to sit next to Princess Hula Hoop since all the other seats are taken." Lexie knew, without even looking across the table, who it was. Her heart started to beat faster. Her hands got sweaty.

Emma eyed the boy as she sipped from her juice pack. "What is your problem, Motor Mouth?" she said crossly.

"Motor Mouth . . ." repeated the boy, like he was testing out the words. He smiled. "I like it. But it's Marcus Motor Mouth to you!"

So now they knew his name. Marcus. And he was not going to scare easily. Emma, Taylor and Lexie watched as he laid out his lunch in a neat row. Cheese and crackers, pudding, a granola bar and apple juice. He looked at Emma's lunch, then Taylor's. He spent a long time checking out Lexie's food. "You eat weird stuff," he announced. Pieces of cracker flew out of his mouth and landed on the table.

Lexie remained silent.

"Didn't you hear me? You deaf, too? I said you eat weird junk."

Lexie glared at Marcus. "No, I don't!" she yelled. "I eat the same stuff as everyone else!"

"Oh, really? Prove it!" Marcus taunted. "Eat *this*." And he shoved the granola bar toward Lexie.

Lexie stared at the bar. Should she?

Marcus sat with his arms crossed over his chest. He wore a smug look on his face.

"I just don't feel like eating a granola bar right now," Lexie replied.

"Chicken," Marcus taunted.

"Am not!"

"Are so!"

Lexie couldn't stand it any longer. She grabbed the bar out of his hand. "Give me that!" she yelled and she began ripping off the wrapper.

"Lexie, don't do it!" begged Taylor.

"It's not on your diet. You'll get sick," Emma cried.

Lexie glared at Marcus. "Watch this." And she shoved the entire granola bar into her mouth. Her cheeks bulged out. She chewed and chewed and chewed until she swallowed the last bite. "Happy?" She scowled.

Marcus gawked at her in disbelief. He looked at the rest of his lunch. Then he stared at Lexie. "I didn't think you'd really do it," he whispered. He looked scared.

Emma grabbed Lexie's arm. This was bad news. "You shouldn't have eaten that," she said.

Taylor tapped Emma on the shoulder. She cupped her hands at Emma's ear. "I think we should tell Ms Sampson," she whispered.

"But I don't want to get Lexie in trouble," Emma whispered back.

"But we have to tell," hissed Taylor. "This is serious."

Emma hung her head and nodded.

After lunch, both girls approached Ms Sampson. She was sitting at her desk, correcting journals. Ms Sampson glanced up and smiled. When she saw the look on Taylor's face, she frowned. "You two are looking pretty serious. Is something wrong?"

"Well . . ." Taylor paused. "We don't want to get anyone in trouble but . . ." Her voice trailed off.

"Lexie ate something she shouldn't have!" Emma blurted out. "In the cafeteria. A few minutes ago."

"Oh, my!" said Ms Sampson. She leaned forward and looked closely at both girls. "Tell me exactly what happened."

Chapter 8

A few minutes later, Lexie found herself standing before Ms Sampson. She hung her head and shuffled her feet back and forth.

"Of course, you know this means I have to call your dad," said Ms Sampson. "Why would you ever do something like this?" She sighed.

"I was just so mad," replied Lexie, in a quiet voice. "For once, I wanted to be like everyone else."

"It must be hard," agreed Ms Sampson. "But you know you can't eat the same food as the other kids." She pointed to a chair. "Have a seat until your father gets here."

Lexie's father arrived thirty minutes later. He did not look happy. "Thank you for calling," he said to Ms Sampson. "Lexie will probably be out of school for a few days until we get her diet under control." He looked at his daughter. "Let's go, kiddo. The car is parked out front."

* * *

When Monday rolled around, Lexie was back on track with her diet and happy to return to school. Home had been boring. Now, she was just in time to hear about Soheil's random act of kindness.

Soheil was at the front of the room. He swayed from side to side as he held the kindness stone first in his right hand, then in his left. He had a big smile on his face.

"In the beginning, I wasn't sure what I was going to do," he admitted. "I wanted to do something really special. But I didn't know what." He paused and looked around the room. "Every week I go with Mom to the nursing home to visit Grammy. It's usually pretty boring. Sometimes Grammy falls asleep while we're talking. But I always take my drawing book with me. In case I get bored."

Soheil paused. A sad look came over his face. "Grammy has a roommate named Mrs. Semple. She wanders up and down the hallway a lot. She never gets any company. So she's reeeeeally lonely. When it was time to go, I left one of my drawings on her table. It was the best one in the book. It was of the *Bluenose*. After we got home, someone from the nursing home phoned my mom and told us that Mrs. Semple had found the drawing right away. She was so happy that she started to cry. She held the picture against her heart and hugged it. Then she put my picture up on her bulletin board. It's the only thing decorating her side of the room."

"How kind of you, Soheil," said Ms Sampson. "What a great way to brighten someone's day. I'm sure you probably felt as good as Mrs. Semple. And I am sure your mom was very proud of you."

Soheil nodded his head.

"This project is turning out better than I had thought. I am so pleased that we are doing it. I think we are truly making people's lives a little bit happier. Now," said Ms Sampson, "who would you like to give the stone to?"

Soheil rolled the stone over and over in his hand. "Who wants it?" he asked the class. He looked at all the kids. "I pick . . . I pick . . ."

Lexie wondered if he would pick another boy. Maybe it would be a girl's turn again. For the kazillionth time she thought, how will I ever do a random act of kindness *and* keep it a secret? Especially when a grownup is always hanging around me.

"I pick . . . Taylor," Soheil announced.

* * *

Taylor had a hard time deciding what to do for her good deed. Now that the weather had turned colder, she hardly ever went to the park. She wouldn't be able to pick up litter and anyway, Brady had already done that. She never got to visit anyone at the nursing home. That meant she couldn't help old people. What could she do? She wracked her brain, searching for an idea. The week was almost up and she still hadn't thought of anything.

Then, at the end of the day on Friday, the perfect situation presented itself.

"Have a great weekend, everyone!" said Ms Sampson, as she waved to her class boarding the buses.

"See you on Monday!" called Taylor, scrambling up the bus steps.

"I didn't think you were coming today," grumbled Mr. Rossignol, the driver. "One of these days you're going to be too late." He scowled at Taylor. "Now take a seat. We're ready to go."

Taylor knew she was late. She was always

the last kid on Bus 75. But Emma had probably saved a seat for her, as usual.

Emma waved from her seat. "Back here, Taylor!" The back was the best place on the bus. When Mr. Rossignol drove over a bump, you practically flew off the seat. It was so much fun!

Taylor made her way down the aisle. The bus was noisy and smelled like sweaty feet and chewing gum. Halfway there, she noticed a little kid sitting by himself. His book bag was almost as big as he was. His feet didn't even reach the floor. And worst of all, he was crying. Taylor paused next to his seat.

"What's wrong?" she asked.

The boy looked at Taylor and said in a teeny voice, "This . . . this . . . is my first time on the bus . . . by myself." He began to cry even harder. He managed to squeak out, "My sister . . . felt sick . . . and Mom got her . . . at lunch." He wiped a runny nose on the back of his sleeve.

"Oh," said Taylor quietly. She remembered

the first time she had had to ride the bus
without her brother. She hadn't cried, but it
had been scary.

She glanced down the aisle. Emma was
frantically waving to her. "Hurry up," she
called.

"I'll sit with you on Monday," Taylor called
back. She pointed to the seat next to the little
boy. "I'm going to sit here."

She slid into the seat. "My name is Taylor,"
she told the boy, smiling. "What's yours?"

The little boy stared at her. He took a long shuddering breath. "Nolan."

"I bet you're in Kindergarten, aren't you?" Taylor said.

"How'd you know that?"

She looked at his dangling feet and the too-big book bag. "Just a guess," she said.

Taylor kept up a conversation for the rest of the bus ride. By the time he got off the bus, Nolan was no longer crying. Taylor had learned that he loved collecting bugs and that his favourite food was pizza. She waved goodbye to him. "See you, Nolan!"

Nolan shyly waved back.

It wasn't until the bus was at the next stop that Taylor sat bolt upright. "Oh, my gosh," she whispered to herself. "It wasn't a secret, but I think I just did my random act of kindness!" She smiled to herself. Ms Sampson was right. It was a terrific feeling.

Chapter 9

Fall quickly turned into winter. One December night, snow blanketed the ground. The weather became icy cold. Week after week, Ms Sampson's Grade Three class found different ways to do random acts of kindness. Stefen shovelled a neighbour's snowy walkway. When Mya's aunt broke her leg, Mya snuck into her yard every morning for a week and scooped her dog's poop. It was a gross job. Sometimes the good deed was quick and easy, like writing a happy message to someone who needed cheering. Of course, Alisa didn't sign the note. Other times the good deed happened unexpectedly — like when Zach filled the empty bird feeder with seeds and nuts during a winter storm.

Throughout it all, Lexie began to worry a little bit less. She thought about doing something easy, like emptying the kitchen compost. Or organizing her toys in the rec room. She knew she could do it, but she wasn't sure how to keep it a secret.

* * *

For one whole week in January, the weather was so cold the kids at Malone Bay Public School had to stay inside for their recess breaks. At first, it was lots of fun. There were puzzles to do and Lego creations to build. Ms Sampson put out new clay and set up a puppet theatre.

"I wish we could go outside," Emma said to Lexie.

"Me too," Taylor agreed. "I'm bored. I want to go tobogganing."

"Maybe we could think of something else to do inside," suggested Lexie.

"Like what?" asked Emma.

Lexie thought hard. At home she had to stay inside lots of times, especially if her dad was too busy to go out with her. She liked to paint and read. But those things were pretty ordinary. Maybe, just maybe, they could do something totally different.

"I could put on a magic show," she said carefully. "I know how to do about ten different tricks."

Emma's eyes grew wide. "You know how to do magic? Really?"

Lexie nodded her head. "Every time I miss school because of my epilepsy, Dad teaches me a new trick. Last summer I even went to a magician's day camp."

Ms Sampson stopped near the girls. "What's this I hear about magic?" she asked.

"Lexie can do magic!" Taylor blurted out.

Ms Sampson faced Lexie. "That's pretty special," she said. "Would you like to show the class one of your tricks?"

Lexie smiled shyly. "Sure. I could bring my stuff in tomorrow."

"That would be wonderful," said Ms Sampson. She looked out the window at the swirling snow. "It will give everyone something to look forward to!"

* * *

The next day, Lexie dragged a shiny blue bag to the front of the room. It was covered with big gold stars. First, she put on her black magician's hat. Then she pulled out four small balls. There was a red one, a blue one, a yellow one and a green one. She faced the class. This was something she was good at.

She tossed the red ball in the air. Then the blue one. Lexie kept tossing the balls in the air until she was juggling all four balls. Round and round they went. And not one fell.

"Wow! How do you do that?" asked Brady.

"Cool," said someone else.

Then one by one, Lexie caught all the balls and held on to them with her right hand. She took a deep bow. The class clapped and cheered.

"For my first trick, I need a volunteer," she announced.

All the hands went up. Everyone wanted to volunteer.

Lexie looked at her friends. "Brady, come on up."

Brady scrambled to the front of the room.

Lexie smiled at Brady. "I am going to read your mind," she said.

She reached into her magician's bag and pulled out a wand and a deck of cards. She handed the cards to Brady. "Shuffle them," she instructed.

Brady shuffled. A few cards fell to the floor. The class giggled. He scooped them up, put them back in the deck and continued shuffling.

"Now," said Lexie, "I want you to pick a card. Any card. But don't tell me what it is."

Brady fanned the deck and picked a card from the middle. He looked at it. "Show the audience what you picked, but don't let me see it."

Brady held the card out and waved it back and forth in front of the class.

"Please put the card back in the deck and shuffle the cards again. And I want you to think about the card." She waved the wand over Brady's head. "Concentrate . . . concentrate . . ." Lexie said the words slowly, over and over. "Now, I will pick the card you are thinking about."

Lexie began flipping over the cards. A jack, a five, a ten, a queen. She flipped faster and faster. "Ahh," she said. "This is it!" And she turned over the seven of hearts.

Brady was amazed. "That's it! How'd you do that?" He scratched his head. "You read my mind!"

Lexie smiled. "It's magic," she said.

Chapter 10

Lexie looked at the class. "I have one more trick I'd like to do this morning," she said. "And I need another volunteer." She scanned the room. "How about you, Ms Sampson?"

Ms Sampson stepped over near Lexie. "Have a seat," Lexie said. She pointed to a nearby chair.

When Ms Sampson sat down, Lexie pulled a coil of rope from her magician's bag. She gripped it with both hands and tugged. "It's a rope, folks. An ordinary rope. Emma," she said, "would you come up here, please?" Emma scooted up to Lexie. "I want you to tie Ms Sampson to the chair. Tie her as tightly as you can." Lexie grinned at the class.

The class began hollering and shouting. This magic show was getting better by the minute.

Lexie noticed that everyone was laughing — everyone except her teacher. She chewed on her bottom lip. She hoped Ms Sampson would be a good sport about this next trick. And she hoped the trick would work. If it didn't, she'd be in trouble. Big trouble.

Emma was too busy wrapping the rope around Ms Sampson's ankles to notice that her teacher was not smiling. Then she tied her wrists together. "She's not going anywhere!" Emma laughed.

Lexie gave a tug on the rope. She nodded

her head. "It looks pretty tight to me." Then she smiled and said, "Okay, Ms Sampson, try to get loose."

Ms Sampson wiggled back and forth. She pulled one way and then the other. The rope remained tied. The class laughed. Ms Sampson looked concerned.

Lexie raised her hand for silence. She moved her wand in circles above Ms Sampson's head. "I will now say the magic words. Abracadabra." She gently tapped her teacher on her wrists where the rope was fastened. Magically, the rope fell away! Lexie tapped her ankles. And presto! The rope dropped to the floor! Ms Sampson was free!

The class clapped. Some kids hooted.

"Amazing," said a relieved Ms Sampson. "How did you do that?"

Lexie smiled. "It's magic," she said. "And a magician never tells."

Ms Sampson laughed. "That was quite the trick."

A crowd gathered around Lexie at recess time. "Teach us how to do magic," the kids begged.

"It takes lots of practice," she explained. "I get to practise when I miss school because of my epilepsy. But here's a pretty easy one. This was the first trick I learned at Magician Camp." Lexie told them how to pull a quarter out of someone's ear. The kids practised hard and by the end of recess, a few of them could almost do it.

"It's fun, but it's really tricky, too." Taylor laughed. "You're good at this."

"Thanks," said Lexie. She grinned. It felt great to be good at something.

* * *

Winter crept by. Almost everyone in the class had done a good deed. Lexie knew that, pretty soon, it would be her turn with the kindness stone.

"I'm not sure what I'll do," she confessed to

Emma one day at recess. The schoolyard was covered in new snow. Kids were busy making forts, sliding down banks and creating snow angels. The girls were building a snowman. Emma had added two spindly sticks for the arms. Lexie was adding the finishing touches — medium-sized rocks for the smile — when she began to feel dizzy.

She knew what was about to happen. She tried to form the words. But she couldn't get them out fast enough. She needed to let Emma know! And then, almost in slow motion, Lexie swayed back and forth and slowly fell to the ground.

When she woke up, Mr. Johnson was kneeling beside her. She was lying on her side. Someone's winter jacket was tucked beneath her head. Emma stood nearby, holding her helmet. She peered down at her, a worried look on her face.

Mr. Johnson was very calm. He smiled at Lexie. "You're okay," he said. "I bet you're feeling tired, though. You just had a seizure. Let's get you inside. Then we'll give your dad a call."

"I'll come in and stay with Lexie until her dad gets here," Emma volunteered.

Mr. Johnson smiled at Emma. "That's very kind of you. It looks as though the Grade Three kindness project is working in lots of ways."

After Lexie went home, Emma said to Ms Sampson, "That was kind of scary. Not as scary as I thought it would be. But still . . ."

"You handled it very well," replied Ms Sampson. "You were a good friend." She looked thoughtful. "I think it's always a bit scary when something like that happens for the first time. Lexie will be back to school on Monday, I'm sure. And everything will be fine."

* * *

But on Monday morning, Lexie told her dad, "I have a pain in my tummy. I don't think I should go to school today."

Dad looked at her half-eaten bacon and the nearly full glass of her special milkshake. "Hmm . . ." He felt her forehead. "Nope," he said, "no fever." He cocked his head to the side, noticing her quivering lip. "Okay," he said, "what's going on?"

Lexie hung her head. She sniffled. "All the kids will think I'm weird." She lowered her voice. Dad had to strain to hear the next words. "They'll think I'm a freak."

"Are you thinking that because of your seizure on Friday?"

Lexie's head bobbed up and down.

"I bet," said Dad, "that your class will just be happy that you're back. Remember, you did a great job explaining epilepsy with your poster. So they know a lot about it." He patted her shoulder. "And don't forget, you have another magic trick to show them. That'll make them happy, right?"

"I guess," Lexie replied.

"Now, let's get ready for school. You need to hurry or you'll miss the bus," said Dad.

But it wasn't missing the bus that worried Lexie. Deep down inside, she still wasn't convinced that everything would be okay.

Chapter 11

The minute Lexie walked through the door of the classroom, Emma ran over to her.

"Look what we're doing today!" she yelled. She waved red paper hearts in the air. "We're making our valentine bags." She grabbed Lexie's arm and dragged her to a table at the front of the room. "And look at all the different kinds of glitter!" Bottles of red, gold and silver glitter were lined up on the table.

Lexie laughed. It seemed as though her dad was right. Everything was going to be okay. A little part of her was surprised that Emma didn't mention her seizure. But an even bigger part of her was happy to be doing a new art project.

After twenty valentine bags were hung, the glitter swept up and paper put away, Ms Sampson announced that it was time for Gaven to talk about his random act of kindness.

Gaven walked to the front of the room. "I decided to do something that was easy." He paused. "Well, I *thought* it was going to be easy. I decided that for one week, I would smile at one hundred people in Malone Bay Public School. Not counting kids in our class. That meant I needed to smile at twenty different people a day. He clutched the stone in his hand. "It was a lot harder than I thought."

Ms Sampson looked thoughtful. "Did you discover anything while doing your project?"

Gaven sighed. "Yes. First, it was really hard to do. But I already said that." Everybody laughed. "And the other thing I noticed is how surprised some people seemed when I smiled at them. It was kind of weird. I smiled at the janitor. I smiled at visitors when they came to the school. I even smiled at Marcus." Gaven lowered his voice. "Everyone knows he's a bully. I think he was the most surprised of all. And . . . I think I made people happy."

"That was a great idea," said Ms Sampson. "Now, why don't you pick someone else to have a turn?"

Gaven looked around the room. He paused and looked directly at Garrett and pointed. "I pick you," he said. He walked over and placed the stone in his hand.

Phew, thought Lexie. Safe for another week.

* * *

It turned out that Lexie was safe for quite a few more weeks. Xavier and Max each had a turn. So did Tait and Ethan. Finally, when Hannah had completed her random act of kindness, there was no one else left to give the stone to. "It's your turn, Lexie," she said.

Lexie rolled the kindness stone over and over in her hand. It felt warm and smooth. Now she had no choice. She needed to come up with an idea. She had exactly one week. Just thinking about it made her mouth feel dry.

Every day Lexie thought about doing something nice for someone else. She thought about it on Monday. She thought about it on Tuesday. On Wednesday night she had a hard time falling asleep. "Tomorrow," she decided, "I'll ask Taylor for some suggestions."

It wasn't that she didn't have any of her own ideas. She had lots. She could make her bed for a week without being reminded. She could buy her father his favourite chocolate bar and put it in his lunch box as a treat. She even thought about washing his truck. They were all good ideas. But she knew her dad would easily figure out who had done it. And, more than anything, Lexie wanted it to be a secret.

On Thursday at recess time, Taylor told her, "Gee, I don't know what you can do." She bounced the basketball up and down before she took a shot on the net. "Mine just sort of happened. A little kid was crying on the bus and I sat down with him. It was easy." A thoughtful look came over her face. "Maybe you're trying too hard."

"Maybe," agreed Lexie. "I know one thing for sure. I'm glad it's Easter weekend. That gives me Monday, too, to do something."

At bus time, Ms Sampson handed out pamphlets. "I almost forgot to pass these out," she said, as she waved the papers in the air. "Here's some information on the annual Malone Bay Easter Egg Hunt. It takes place on Saturday at the community park." She waved goodbye to everyone as they climbed onto the bus. "Have a great weekend!" she called.

"I found seventeen eggs last year," Taylor told Lexie. They were sitting on the bus, waiting for Mr. Rossignol to leave the schoolyard. Taylor laughed out loud as she remembered some of the strange places she had found the plastic eggs at the park. "Lots were in the grass. Some were behind rocks. I even found one in a tree!"

"That sounds like fun." Lexie smiled at her friend. "I'm going to ask Dad if I can go."

As soon as she got home, Lexie passed her dad the pamphlet. "Can we go to the Easter Egg Hunt? Taylor and Emma are going. Everybody's going! It'll be lots of fun!"

"That sounds like a good idea to me," he said.

* * *

The day of the egg hunt was cloudy and cool. It looked as if it was going to rain. Lexie crossed her fingers. "No rain, no rain," she whispered to herself.

She bundled up in an extra warm jacket.

She wondered how many eggs she would be able to find. She knew she would make sure to look up in the trees and check behind rocks.

When she got to the park, a lady dressed like a giant bunny gave her a basket. "You can collect your eggs in this," she explained. She pointed to a big group of kids. "You can wait over there until it's time to start."

There were tons of kids at the park. Some were older than Lexie. Some were younger. But most of them were about her age. She spotted

Taylor on the opposite side of the field and waved. Then she noticed someone nearby. She nudged her dad. "Dad," she whispered. "Why is that boy wearing sunglasses?" She glanced up at the sky. It was filled with heavy black clouds. It looked like it could rain any second.

Dad looked at the boy. "See the white cane? I think he's blind. Maybe not totally, but he at least has a hard time seeing."

Lexie was puzzled. "How will he ever find any eggs?" she asked.

"I don't know," answered Dad. "It will be hard, that's for sure."

Before Dad could say anything else, the lady in the rabbit outfit stepped up to a microphone. "Welcome, everyone, to Malone Bay's Fifth Annual Easter Egg Hunt! Is everyone ready?"

"Yes! Yes!" the kids shouted.

"Okay," announced the lady. "Five, four, three, two, one . . . start hunting!"

Lexie dashed out into the field. Right away she found a blue egg in the grass. She found a purple one behind a rock. She filled her basket with more and more plastic eggs — green ones, pink ones and yellow ones. She didn't find any in trees, but she did find two in the bird bath.

The boy with the sunglasses was crouched next to her near a hedge. Lexie looked in his basket. Only one egg.

Behind him, a woman said, "Move your hand a bit to the left, Robbie!"

Lexie watched as Robbie's hand searched through the grass, just missing the egg.

"You almost have it," encouraged the woman. "Keep searching!"

Lexie stopped hunting for eggs. She watched Robbie reach out, trying over and over to find the egg. It was right there, in plain sight. He was just about to touch the egg, when a big kid reached down and scooped it up.

"Found another one!" the big kid yelled and then he ran off down the field.

"Oh, dear," exclaimed the woman. "We

missed that one. Let's move a bit to the left."
She passed Robbie his cane. He walked a few
steps. "Try here."

Lexie could see the disappointment on the
woman's face.

Robbie got down on his hands and knees.
He reached out, sweeping his fingers through
the grass. Finally, after a long time, he touched
a pink egg. "I found one!" he shrieked. And
he carefully placed it in his basket.

Lexie looked at her basket. She had tons of
eggs. She looked at the two eggs in Robbie's
basket. He was back on his hands and knees,
searching for the next one.

Lexie reached in her basket and dropped a
yellow egg beside Robbie.

She watched as he reached out and touched
the egg. "I found another one!" he yelled.

The woman looked over at Lexie and smiled.
Silently she mouthed the words, "thank you."
Lexie smiled back. She reached in her basket
and dropped another egg not far from Robbie.
She smiled when he found it.

"Here's another one! What colour is it, Mom?"

"Green," answered the woman.

"I'm getting good at this," Robbie squealed. "You said this wasn't a good idea, Mom. But look! It's easy!"

Next Lexie dropped a purple egg. Then another yellow one. And Robbie found every one of them. Her basket was almost empty when Taylor ran over.

"Hey, you hardly have any eggs," she said "Look at mine!" She held out her basket. It was filled with eggs of every colour.

"I have enough." Lexie smiled. She dropped the last egg near Robbie.

Taylor watched as Robbie searched the grass. She noticed the dark sunglasses and the woman holding the white cane. "Oh," she said softly.

"Found one!" yelled Robbie. He added another egg to his collection.

Taylor looked at her full basket again. Then she looked at Robbie, who was still hunting for more eggs. But there were no more eggs for him to find. Lexie's basket was empty. "I get it," she whispered. Then Taylor quietly placed a blue egg near Robbie.

It was at that exact moment that Lexie knew. She had done it! She had just completed her random act of kindness. It hadn't been planned. It just happened. Kind of by accident.

Chapter 12

Lexie rubbed the kindness stone between her fingers as the bus bounced along the road to school. The smoothness of it felt comforting. She thought about the Easter weekend, the egg hunt and Robbie. It had been so much fun. Helping others felt good.

"Welcome back," said Ms Sampson when she walked through the door. "Did you have a good weekend?"

Lexie nodded her head. "The best!" She smiled at the teacher. "I even did my random act of kindness."

"That's wonderful! I knew you could do it," said Ms Sampson. "I'm looking forward to hearing all about it."

Lexie grinned. She thought about the

months and months she had worried over what she was going to do. She thought about trying to fit in. And she realized that she, Lexie Peters, was able to do things just like anyone else.

She put the stone on Ms Sampson's desk. "I'm ready!"

* * *

". . . and that's what I did," finished Lexie. She smiled at the class.

Taylor gave her a thumbs up.

"Awesome," said Gaven. "That was way better than mine."

"What a good idea," added Emma.

Ms Sampson stood up. "They were all great ideas. Grade Three, I am so proud of you. With the help of the kindness stone, I challenged you to make the world a better place, and you did! I think we can consider our project on random acts of kindness a huge success. And remember, you can practise kindness anywhere, any time. Even the tiniest deed can make a big difference in someone else's life. You found that out." She looked around at all the kids. "You know . . ." She paused.

The class waited.

Ms Sampson rolled the kindness stone thoughtfully between her fingers. Her bracelets jingled. She began again, "You know . . ." Her voice trailed off. She laughed.

"What?" yelled the class.

"We still have two and a half months of school left. I think we might have *just* enough time left to do another little project." She lowered her voice. "We'll keep it a secret until June. But I think we should . . ."

The kids all leaned forward in their seats, straining to hear. Everyone knew it would be something fun. But, with Ms Sampson, you never knew what it would be.

Also by
Nancy Wilcox Richards